Beyond Pretty

Written by B. C. Hatch
Illusrated by Victor Marc

Printed in the United States of
America
First Edition, 2018

ISBN: 978-1-948682-00-8 (Hardback)
ISBN: 978-1-948682-01-5 (Paperback)
ISBN: 978-1-948682-02-2 (E-book)

Little ChickLit
P.O. Box 37942
Jacksonville, FL 32205

www.LittleChickLit.com

For Thea

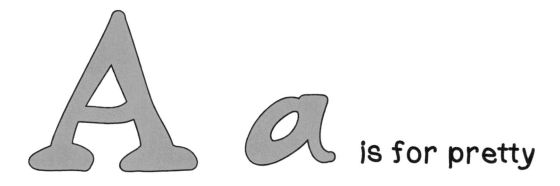**is for pretty**

Ambitious

Determined girls who
work hard to succeed.

B b is for pretty

Brave

Girls who don't back down
even if they're afraid.

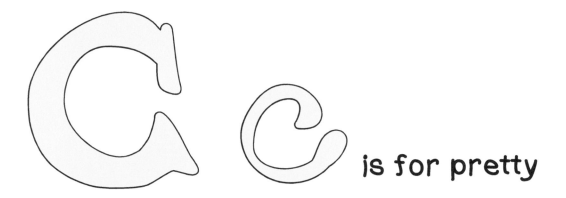 is for pretty

If you're in need they're
the first to assist.

 is for pretty

Adventurous girls
who take risks.

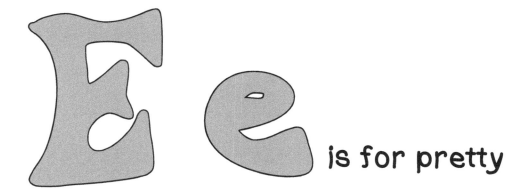 **is for pretty**

Energetic

These girls hardly
ever slow down.

 is for pretty

Funny

The comedians and
the class clowns.

G g is for pretty

Gregarious

These girls love to
mingle in groups.

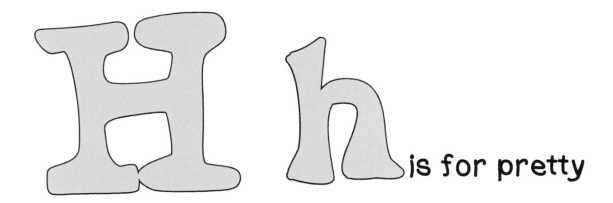 is for pretty

Honest

Girls who always
tell the truth.

I i

is for pretty

Inventive

Creative girls full of
grand new ideas.

J j

is for pretty

Joyous

These girls are cheery,
upbeat, and gleeful.

 is for pretty

Knowledgeable

Girls who are educated,
well-read and informed.

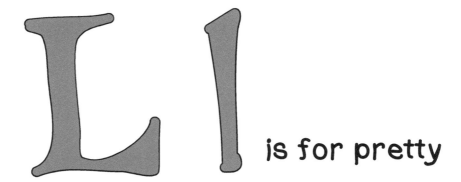 is for pretty

Logical

Girls who make sure every
possibility gets explored.

One more letter

and we'll be half way through.

Are any of these girls like you?

Perhaps not one, but two, or three;

there are endless possibilities.

So many still we'll likely miss

with all the options that exist,

but let's read on and try our best,

to name a few more with the letters left.

Now where were we?

A B C D E F

GHIJKL

 is for pretty

Magnanimous

Girls who are forgiving
when others aren't nice.

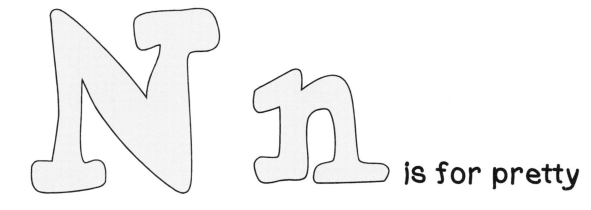 is for pretty

Noble

Girls who are always
careful to do what is right.

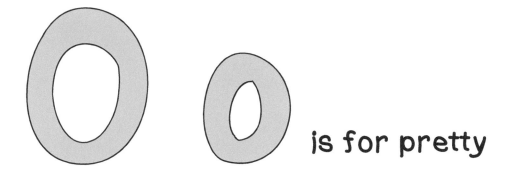 is for pretty

Organized

For these girls
everything has a place.

P p

is for pretty

Poised

Girls who remain composed
and are full of grace.

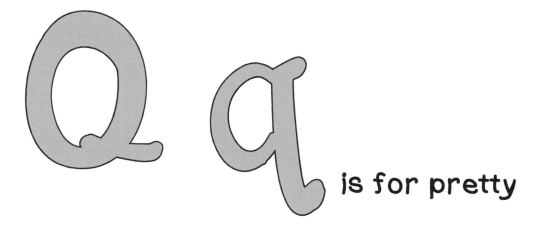 is for pretty

Quirky

These girls are
original and unique.

R r is for pretty

Resourceful

Girls who find clever solutions
when faced with difficulties.

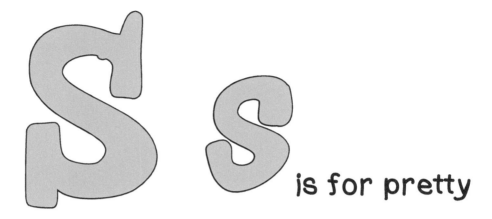 is for pretty

Strong

These girls display
great might.

Tt

is for pretty

_____

Tenacious

Girls who are persistent,
strong willed, and untiring.

 is for pretty

Urbane

Girls who are
sophisticated and refined.

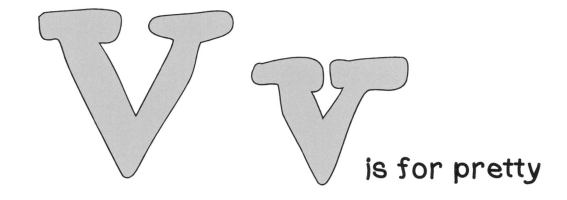

V v is for pretty

Visionary

The girls who help
make the future bright.

There you have

M N O P

Q R S

T U and V

There's only four more letters left;

do you know which one is NEXT?

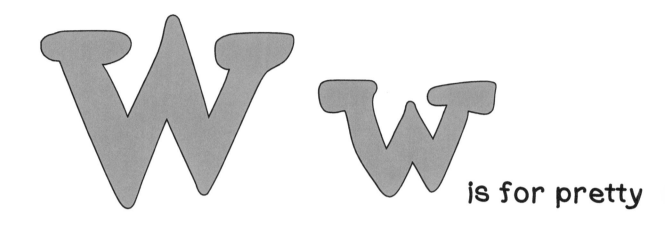

W w is for pretty

Wild

Girls that are enthusiastic,
extreme, and excited.

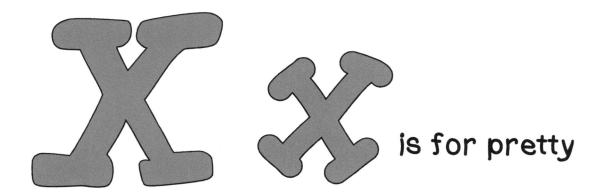 is for pretty

Xenial

It's as hosts that these girls truly shine.
They are welcoming and friendly,
especially to strangers and foreigners
who suddenly arrive.

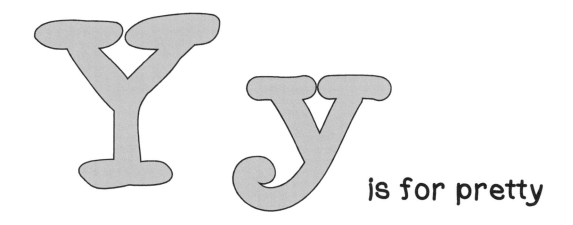 is for pretty

_____

YES I CAN!

All girls have a little of this.

Now last but not least
(simply equal)
we come to the letter Z...

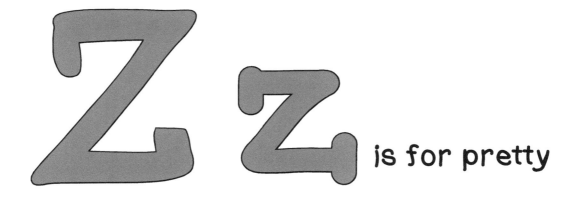 is for pretty

Zirlzazzolorific

Do you know what it means?

O.K. you caught me.
I made it up,
but since I did
and now it exists,
I'll define it as
all of the
WONDERFUL
things girls are
BEYOND PRETTY.